D0591228

Poems from
Child's Garden of Verses

ROBERT LOUIS STEVENSON

Illustrated by Caroline Sharpe

FREDERICK WARNE

FREDERICK WARNE
Penguin Books Ltd, 27 Wrights Lane, London W8 5TZ (Publishing and E
and Harmondsworth, Middlesex, England (Distribution and Warehou
Viking Penguin Inc., 40 West 23rd Street, New York, New York 10010,
Penguin Books Australia Ltd, Ringwood, Victoria, Australia
Penguin Books Canada Ltd, 2801 John Street, Markham, Ontario, Canada
Penguin Books (NZ) Ltd, 182–190 Wairau Road, Auckland 10, New Zea

First published 1885
This edition first published 1987
Selection and format copyright © Frederick Warne & Co., 1987
Illustrations copyright © Caroline Sharpe, 1987

ISBN 0-7232-3525-2

Printed and bound in Great Britain by William Clowes Limited,
Beccles and London

CONTENTS

BED IN SUMMER

In winter I get up at night
And dress by yellow candle-light.
In summer, quite the other way,
I have to go to bed by day.

I have to go to bed and see
The birds still hopping on the tree,
Or hear the grown-up people's feet
Still going past me in the street.

And does it not seem hard to you,
When all the sky is clear and blue,
And I should like so much to play,
To have to go to bed by day?

AT THE SEASIDE

When I was down beside the sea
A wooden spade they gave to me
    To dig the sandy shore.
My holes were empty like a cup,
In every hole the sea came up
    Till it could come no more.

YOUNG NIGHT THOUGHT

All night long, and every night,
When my mamma puts out the light,
I see the people marching by,
As plain as day, before my eye.

Armies and emperors and kings,
All carrying different kinds of things,
And marching in so grand a way,
You never saw the like by day.

6

So fine a show was never seen
At the great circus on the green;
For every kind of beast and man
Is marching in that caravan.

At first they move a little slow,
But still the faster on they go,
And still beside them close I keep
Until we reach the town of Sleep.

FOREIGN LANDS

Up into the cherry-tree
Who should climb but little me?
I held the trunk with both my hands
And looked abroad on foreign lands.

I saw the next-door garden lie,
Adorned with flowers before my eye,
And many pleasant places more
That I had never seen before.

I saw the dimpling river pass
And be the sky's blue looking-glass;
The dusty roads go up and down
With people tramping in to town.

If I could find a higher tree
Farther and farther I should see,
To where the grown-up river slips
Into the sea among the ships,

To where the roads on either hand
Lead onward into fairy land,
Where all the children dine at five,
And all the playthings come alive.

WHOLE DUTY OF CHILDREN

A child should always say what's true,
And speak when he is spoken to,
And behave mannerly at table:
At least as far as he is able.

RAIN

The rain is raining all around,
　　It falls on field and tree,
It rains on the umbrellas here,
　　And on the ships at sea.

WINDY NIGHTS

Whenever the moon and stars are set,
  Whenever the wind is high,
All night long in the dark and wet,
  A man goes riding by.
Late in the night when the fires are out,
Why does he gallop and gallop about?

Whenever the trees are crying aloud,
  And ships are tossed at sea,
By, on the highway, low and loud,
  By at the gallop goes he.
By at the gallop he goes, and then
By he comes back at the gallop again.

13

SINGING

Of speckled eggs the birdie sings
    And nests among the trees;
The sailor sings of ropes and things
    In ships upon the seas.

The children sing in far Japan,
    The children sing in Spain;
The organ with the organ man
    Is singing in the rain.

A GOOD PLAY

We built a ship upon the stairs
All made of the back-bedroom chairs,
And filled it full of sofa pillows
To go a-sailing on the billows.

We took a saw and several nails,
And water in the nursery pails;
And Tom said, 'Let us also take
An apple and a slice of cake';
Which was enough for Tom and me
To go a-sailing on, till tea.

We sailed along for days and days,
And had the very best of plays;
But Tom fell out and hurt his knee,
So there was no one left but me.

WHERE GO THE BOATS?

Dark brown is the river,
    Golden is the sand.
It flows along for ever,
    With trees on either hand.

Green leaves a-floating,
    Castles of the foam,
Boats of mine a-boating –
    Where will all come home?

On goes the river
    And out past the mill,
Away down the valley,
    Away down the hill.

Away down the river,
    A hundred miles or more,
Other little children
    Shall bring my boats ashore.

THE LAND OF COUNTERPANE

When I was sick and lay a-bed,
I had two pillows at my head,
And all my toys beside me lay
To keep me happy all the day.

And sometimes for an hour or so
I watched my leaden soldiers go,
With different uniforms and drills,
Among the bed-clothes, through the
    hills;

And sometimes sent my ships in fleets
All up and down among the sheets;
Or brought my trees and houses out,
And planted cities all about.

I was the giant great and still
That sits upon the pillow-hill,
And sees before him, dale and plain,
The pleasant land of counterpane.

MY SHADOW

I have a little shadow that goes in and out
      with me,
And what can be the use of him is more
      than I can see.
He is very, very like me from the heels up
      to the head;
And I see him jump before me, when I
      jump into my bed.

The funniest thing about him is the way he
      likes to grow –
Not at all like proper children, which is
      always very slow;
For he sometimes shoots up taller like an
      india-rubber ball,
And he sometimes gets so little that there's
      none of him at all.

He hasn't got a notion of how children
　　ought to play,
And can only make a fool of me in every
　　sort of way.
He stays so close beside me, he's a cowar
　　you can see;
I'd think shame to stick to nursie as that
　　shadow sticks to me!

One morning, very early, before the sun
     was up,
I rose and found the shining dew on every
     buttercup;
But my lazy little shadow, like an arrant
     sleepy-head,
Had stayed at home behind me and was fast
     asleep in bed.

THE COW

The friendly cow, all red and white,
   I love with all my heart:
She gives me cream with all her might,
   To eat with apple-tart.

She wanders lowing here and there,
   And yet she cannot stray,
All in the pleasant open air,
   The pleasant light of day;

And blown by all the winds that pass
   And wet with all the showers,
She walks among the meadow grass
   And eats the meadow flowers.

ESCAPE AT BEDTIME

The lights from the parlour and kitchen
    shone out
  Through the blinds and the windows
    and bars;
And high overhead and all moving about,
  There were thousands of millions of stars
There ne'er were such thousands of leaves
    on a tree,
  Nor of people in church or the Park,
As the crowds of the stars that looked
    down upon me,
  And that glittered and winked in the
    dark.

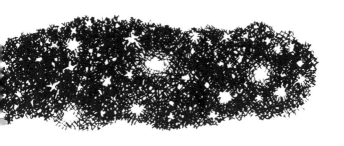

The Dog, and the Plough, and the Hunter,
    and all,
  And the star of the sailor, and Mars,
These shone in the sky, and the pail by
    the wall
  Would be half full of water and stars.
They saw me at last, and they chased me
    with cries,
  And they soon had me packed into bed;
But the glory kept shining and bright in
    my eyes,
  And the stars going round in my
    head.

THE MOON

The moon has a face like the clock in the h
She shines on thieves on the garden wall,
On streets and fields and harbour quays,
And birdies asleep in the forks of the trees

The squalling cat and the squeaking mous
The howling dog by the door of the house
The bat that lies in bed at noon,
All love to be out by the light of the moon.

But all of the things that belong to the day
Cuddle to sleep to be out of her way;
And flowers and children close their eyes
Till up in the morning the sun shall rise.

29

GOOD AND BAD CHILDREN

Children, you are very little,
And your bones are very brittle;
If you would grow great and stately,
You must try to walk sedately.

You must still be bright and quiet,
And content with simple diet;
And remain, through all bewild'ring,
Innocent and honest children.

Happy hearts and happy faces,
Happy play in grassy places –
That was how, in ancient ages,
Children grew to kings and sages.

THE LAMPLIGHTER

My tea is nearly ready
    and the sun has left the sky;
It's time to take the window
    to see Leerie going by;
For every night at tea-time
    and before you take your seat,
With lantern and with ladder
    he comes posting up the street.

Now Tom would be a driver
    and Maria go to sea,
And my papa's a banker
    and as rich as he can be;
But I, when I am stronger
    and can choose what I'm to do,
O Leerie, I'll go round at night
    and light the lamps with you!

For we are very lucky,
    with a lamp before the door,
And Leerie stops to light it
    as he lights so many more;
And O! before you hurry by
    with ladder and with light,
O Leerie, see a little child
    and nod to him to-night!

HAPPY THOUGHT

The world is so full
   of a number of things,
I'm sure we should all
   be as happy as kings.

THE WIND

I saw you toss the kites on high
And blow the birds about the sky;
And all around I heard you pass,
Like ladies' skirts across the grass –
     O wind, a-blowing all day long,
     O wind, that sings so loud a song!

I saw the different things you did,
But always you yourself you hid.
I felt you push, I heard you call,
I could not see yourself at all –
     O wind, a-blowing all day long,
     O wind, that sings so loud a song!

O you that are so strong and cold,
O blower, are you young or old?
Are you a beast of field and tree,
Or just a stronger child than me?
     O wind, a-blowing all day long,
     O wind, that sings so loud a song!

THE SWING

How do you like to go up in a swing,
   Up in the air so blue?
Oh, I do think it the pleasantest thing
   Ever a child can do!

Up in the air and over the wall,
   Till I can see so wide,
Rivers and trees and cattle and all
   Over the countryside –

Till I look down on the garden green,
   Down on the roof so brown –
Up in the air I go flying again,
   Up in the air and down!

TIME TO RISE

A birdie with a yellow bill
Hopped upon the window sill.
Cocked his shining eye and said:
'Ain't you 'shamed, you sleepy-head?'

FAIRY BREAD

Come up here, O dusty feet!
  Here is fairy bread to eat.
Here in my retiring room,
  Children, you may dine
On the golden smell of broom
  And the shade of pine;
And when you have eaten well,
Fairy stories hear and tell.

WINTER-TIME

Late lies the wintry sun a-bed,
A frosty, fiery sleepy-head;
Blinks but an hour or two; and then,
A blood-red orange, sets again.

Before the stars have left the skies,
At morning in the dark I rise;
And shivering in my nakedness,
By the cold candle, bathe and dress.

Close by the jolly fire I sit
To warm my frozen bones a bit;
Or with a reindeer-sled, explore
The colder countries round the door.

When, to go out, my nurse doth wrap
Me in my comforter and cap:
The cold wind burns my face, and blows
Its frosty pepper up my nose.

Black are my steps on silver sod;
Thick blows my frosty breath abroad;
And tree and house, and hill and lake,
Are frosted like a wedding-cake.

THE HAYLOFT

Through all the pleasant meadow-side
    The grass grew shoulder-high,
Till the shining scythes went far and wide
    And cut it down to dry.

These green and sweetly smelling drops
    They led in waggons home;
And they piled them here in mountain top
    For mountaineers to roam.

Here is Mount Clear, Mount Rusty-Nail,
    Mount Eagle and Mount High; –
The mice that in these mountains dwell,
    No happier are than I!

O what a joy to clamber there,
    O what a place for play,
With the sweet, the dim, the dusty air,
    The happy hills of hay.

FROM A RAILWAY CARRIAGE

Faster than fairies, faster than witches,
Bridges and houses, hedges and ditches;
And charging along like troops in a battle,
All through the meadows the horses and
    cattle:
All of the sights of the hill and the plain
Fly as thick as driving rain;
And ever again, in the wink of an eye,
Painted stations whistle by.

Here is a child who clambers and scrambles,
All by himself and gathering brambles;
Here is a tramp who stands and gazes;
And there is the green for stringing the
    daisies!
Here is a cart run away in the road
Lumping along with man and load;
And here is a mill, and there is a river:
Each a glimpse and gone for ever!

FAREWELL TO THE FARM

The coach is at the door at last;
The eager children, mounting fast
And kissing hands, in chorus sing:
Good-bye, good-bye, to everything!

To house and garden, field and lawn,
The meadow-gates we swang upon,
To pump and stable, tree and swing,
Good-bye, good-bye, to everything!

And fare you well for evermore,
O ladder at the hayloft door,
O hayloft where the cobwebs cling,
Good-bye, good-bye, to everything!

Crack goes the whip, and off we go;
The trees and houses smaller grow;
Last, round the woody turn we swing:
Good-bye, good-bye, to everything!

WARNE CLASSICS SERIES